HANSEL
&
GRETEL

USA TODAY BESTSELLING AUTHORS

WINTERS &
AMELIA WILDE

NEVER HAVE
I EVER

EVERYONE KNOWS THE TALE
OF HANSEL AND GRETEL.

The innocence that was taken from them and the
torture the witch put them through.
But what happened after they burned the witch in
the oven?

With scars and memories of horror, their lives were
forever changed, until one day the trail leads back to
that cottage in the woods...

1
GRETEL

*O*nce upon a time, I fell in love with a boy.

That was before the curse started. After we killed the witch who kept us captive and thought we'd be safe. We were wrong.

The first hardship to strike our small town was the famine. Crops struggled to grow. The plants that managed to push themselves above the soil were weak and withered. Most of the harvest died in the fields, eaten by insects or infested with blight. The townsfolk kept smiles on their faces in the beginning, reassuring one another that it was only an unlucky year—that the next harvest would be bountiful, and we would forget how hungry we'd gotten.

We replanted the crops the next spring, and for a while, it seemed like all would be well again.

Everyone in the village took turns guarding the fields from pests, saying prayers over the budding plants whenever we could. Spring turned the countryside green around us, and as the weather warmed, people started to have faith once again, satisfied that the worst was over.

But the weather didn't stop warming. Spring became a hot, dry summer, with the earth crumbling under our feet and coating everything into dust. The crops would survive, we thought, as long as we kept the fields watered.

But no well would be deep enough. There aren't enough buckets in the world, or hands to carry them, to protect every inch.

The wildfire came from the forest. It tore through the fields, destroying every last crop. It's hard to deny that we brought the famine. It was on everyone's mind, I'm sure. The witch wasn't dead and her curse would never be forgotten.

The small town sifted through the ashes, looking for seeds, or new growth. *Anything* that would serve as a sign we were meant to live. That we could recover. Two unlucky years surely wouldn't become a pattern. No God could be so cruel.

I don't know which God was watching over our

village. If any deity looked over our village, he couldn't have been kind.

I was in love *before* the hardships. Before the barren fields and hot winds and bitter winters. Before my stomach pinched with hunger and my mouth got dry with thirst.

Before, when all he wanted was taffy, and all I wanted was a cool drink of water on a warm summer day. When all I wanted in the world was to see him smile.

Hansel, the boy who survived hell with me. The boy who I watched become a man. A man I loved. A man I could never have.

His smile was like a clear spring running through the forest and a lush field brimming with crops. It was like sneaking away to pick flowers in the meadow. It was a smile full of promises and secrets, and he gave it to me like I was fresh rain and sunshine.

And all I had to do to see it was knock on the wooden door to his house. He'd answer with a smile, and I couldn't help smiling back.

That was *years* ago. Before the witch. Now we're left with the barren after.

I wish I could go back. I wish I could keep the crops in the fields and snuff out the fire with my fingers before it could burn everything down. I wish I could stop what happened before we ever set foot on that long, dirt road by the old farms.

Before we ever found the witch's house.

But I can't.

I can't change the past.

I can't change that he hates me now.

And I can't stop what's already started.

I stand outside that wooden door, the paint chipped and scratched and the winter wind whistling through my clothes. No matter how many layers I wear, the frigid air goes straight to my skin. It's so cold that my teeth ache. My cheeks burn from the blistering cold.

I can't count how many times I fell asleep dreaming about being in this very spot. It always held possibility for me. The moment before I knocked on this door was always like the moment before opening a gift—giddy anticipation that I knew would be followed by delight.

Now, outside Hansel's door, I wish I was standing anywhere else.

I swallow thickly, trying not to think of all of his smiles. Isn't there any other way through this?

There isn't. I know there isn't. I was up half the

night pacing and trying to think of some other solution. In the end, I came up with nothing.

I wish I didn't have to tell him.

I must, though. I owe him that at least.

And...

I don't think I can stop this by myself. I wish I could. More than anything, I wish I didn't need him, but I do. It's always been him for me.

The hairs on the back of my neck stand, and I cast a look over my shoulder. Is somebody watching?

I can't see a single soul.

That doesn't mean much. The town has been blanketed in thick, ever-present fog for weeks, and it's only been made worse by the winter. White snow piles up everywhere, hiding the shape of the land and houses underneath. If the fog gets any thicker...

I turn back to the door, taking deep breaths to calm myself. It's hard to breathe in the cold and the fog. The air's too thick and heavy. My heart beats harder from my nerves.

It's just Hansel's house. I've knocked on his door a hundred times before. I already know he won't smile at me. I already know where we stand.

The witch changed everything. We killed her and with it, we killed what innocence we had.

Just knock, I think. *Before you freeze to death.*

I take a half-step back and stare at the house instead. I bet the straw roof still leaks in the corner with all this snow. In fact, I imagine it's much worse now, like the paint on the door. It's lost almost all its color. It was red once, but now it's a dull brown. The water wheel on the side of the old house doesn't move. It's frozen solid.

My breath turns white and disappears into the fog in front of my face.

I wish I could disappear like the warmth.

I clench my fists inside the folds of my cloak. There can't be any blood in my fingers, but I can't make myself let go. Every muscle in my body is stiff.

I close my eyes and imagine I'm *gone.* Vanished.

Just like the magic vanished. The good magic. The spells that fixed problems like leaky roofs and barren fields.

Not the magic from *her.* The baneful kind. The kind that changed everything forever and ruined what little goodness I had in my heart. It ruined all the goodness Hansel ever was.

When we killed her, a curse was placed on this village. One we can never escape. One I regret and I'm certain he does too.

My teeth chatter together, and I take a deep

breath like I'm about to dive into the swimming hole at the first sign of spring. It's going to be awful, just like jumping into cold water, but then I'll have done it.

I unclench my fist and raise my hand to knock.

Before I can touch the door, it opens a crack, revealing Hansel.

He doesn't smile at me.

His expression is grim through the crack he's left. Hansel stopped opening it wide for me years ago.

Hansel's mouth curls with distaste. "Gretel."

He says my name with such hate.

At first, I think that must be what warms me. It sends heat through my body. *At least he feels strongly,* I think frantically. *At least he thinks of me at all. If he can hate me, maybe he can—*

No. It's not heat from the way he says my name. It's warmth coming from inside the house. My heart sinks and the reality of what has come of us and the village is inescapable. Hansel and his father have managed to keep their small house warm for the time being.

Hansel looks warm, too—or he would, if it wasn't for the ice in his eyes. The boy I used to know has grown into a man. He's tamed his dark hair and filled out his shirts. A shiver wracks me at the sight of his strong arms, and my teeth chatter harder. I try to get them to stop. It's no use.

I'd thought of what to say on the lonely walk to Hansel's doorstep, but now I can't think of any words that aren't *please don't hate me* and *I'm sorry I ruined everything.* My jaw hurts from how hard my teeth knock together.

I came here for a reason, not to fall apart on the doorstep.

"The witch is back," I blurt, the words spilling from my mouth before I can stop them.

Hansel narrows his eyes and starts to shut the door. The mere mention of what was is met with disdain.

As quick as I can, I shove my hand on the wood to stop him. It's worse than ice. My hand shakes on the wood. "Hansel, please. Could I come in?"

I can barely speak, but I will stand outside and tell him, if that's what I must do.

"Come in, Gretel," a second voice calls. The words are followed by a dry, wracking cough. The sound echoes in the small home. *His father.*

I put my foot between the door and the door-frame and look up into Hansel's eyes. He glares down into mine, holding the door halfway shut. It presses into the arch of my boot.

I raise my eyebrows at him. *You heard your father.*

He glares harder. *I don't care.*

But then his father coughs again, and Hansel gives an annoyed huff and opens the door a little farther. I have to squeeze through, my arm scraping the door, but I make it. Hansel shuts the door behind me with a loud *thud*, dampening the howl of the wind.

The kitchen, the table, the chairs by the fire—all of it is the same as the last time I was here, years ago, before we left for the forest. Before the witch. Only it's weathered and worn now. The rug near the hearth is frayed at the edges. Hansel's father coughs into a cloth in his hand, gripping the armrest of his chair.

At least they have a fire. It crackles in the grate, throwing heat into the rest of the house. I'm grateful for it. The winter is unkind and bitter.

My cloak traps the cold close to my body, so I take it off with shaking hands and turn to hang it on a hook by the door.

Hansel glares at me.

I stare back until he moves out of the way.

Once my cloak is hung up, I swing my bag off my shoulder and hang that up, too. Freed of my few possessions, I make my way across the sparsely furnished room to where Hansel's father is getting out of his chair. I put my hand under his arm and help him to his feet.

"What can I get for you? Water?"

He waves me off, which sends him into another coughing fit.

"Tea," he barks finally, and takes a threadbare cloth from the mantel and lifts the kettle off its hook over the fire. I help him to the table, where he prepares a pot of tea, which he lifts up and shows to us both. "Warm up," he orders. "I have to rest."

"Let me help you." I step forward instantly.

"I'll be all right." Hansel's father puts his hand on my shoulder and squeezes. His eyes are sympathetic, though he's the one who doesn't seem well at all. "Good to see you, Gretel."

His breathing is labored on his way to the bedroom, and once he closes the door, the coughing starts up again.

I turn around to pour the the tea, and Hansel blocks me.

"I'm sorry," I say, looking up to find his eyes black with hatred. "I wouldn't have come if I hadn't—"

"You *shouldn't* have come." He lets go of my wrist like I burned him. "But here you are. What do you want?" I can't deny that it pains me, to see him struggle so. To know what became of the village. I was able to flee, but Hansel couldn't.

I drop my hand to my side. I'd wanted to talk. To tell him how sorry I am, and how I *know* it's been difficult. I'd wanted to sit together the way we used to.

That's not going to happen now.

"I need you to come with me. You—you remember what she said before we did what we did. Before we did what had to be done." A chill runs through my body. It's like a confession. One only he would understand the weight of.

Hansel crosses his arms over his chest. His face is so unfamiliar to me like this. It's like looking at a stranger. "Before we killed her. The witch is dead."

"Hansel. She's come back. I *know* she has. I can feel it." My heart pounds. The witch isn't here—I can see that with my own two eyes—but I'm still terrified. "Something's happened, and I'm scared."

Years ago, he would have taken my hand. He would have asked me what he could do to help me feel less afraid, and then Hansel would have done it.

His expression doesn't change. The hardness that stares back at me is unbearable.

"She can't come back," he says flatly. "If she could,

we'd be dead by now. We'd hear her. The screech-ing." His eyes go dull and faraway. *Hollow.*

I would give anything to go back to when his eyes were bright. *Anything.* But there's no magic that will take me there. I curl my hands into loose fists to keep myself from reaching for Hansel.

"She cast a spell when they killed her."

He looks away, his shoulders tensing, then looks back at me. "That was long ago. Why do you think she's back now?"

I pace in the small kitchen and whisper, "I had a nightmare." It makes my stomach hurt to think about it. The dark path. The black branches covering the sky. The sounds in the forest all around us. "I thought it was real. I thought I was back there."

"A dream doesn't mean—"

"And when I woke *up*," I interrupt, too loud, the dream back in my head. It's not easy to shake it off and keep going. "There were rocks leading to my door."

Hansel scoffs. "Someone else could have—"

I step closer and lower my voice, but I want to scream. "They didn't stay outside the door!"

"So you brought them *in*?"

"I didn't! I—" I glance at the bedroom door. It's still closed. "Either I'm going crazy, or she's beckoning me back. I'm *scared*." We left the small rocks to find our way back home. The rocks have come back to haunt me. Every night for over a week.

"You're going crazy if you think—"

"She's been leaving rocks in my living room! Exactly like the ones we left so we could find our way back! Straight to my door. Beckoning me here!"

His mouth drops open. "What?"

"I swear. They're the same stones." The chill captures my body and it has nothing to do with the winter outside.

Hansel shakes his head. "Stop it." For a moment, his eyes flash. I know the pain he went through. He took the brunt of it. He saved me. He was everything I needed and then he decided we were nothing. Nothing but the past.

"I wish I could. I wish it would stop. But it's not stopping. It's been happening for weeks."

"*Stop* it, Gretel. I don't know why you came here, but it's not—"

"I came here for this," I hiss at him. "Because this is happening, and I can't stop it without you. And I thought you deserved to know. She's not gone. She's back," I warn him with tears pricking my eyes. I wish it wasn't so. But the fear is unrelenting. "I wouldn't come, unless I had no choice."

He leans in, his jaw set and his eyes narrowed, radiating fury. My heart races until I think it'll explode. I'm terrified he'll send me away and shut the door behind me, but I'm also hopeful. Hansel's face is full of fear and anger, but he's *looking* at me. He heard what I came here to tell him.

I think, for a second or two, that he might even touch me. This is the closest we've been in years.

Hansel seems to recognize that at the same time I do.

He takes a sharp step back and huffs out a breath, then looks away, getting control of himself. Hansel relaxes his shoulders, his hands clenching and unclenching at his sides.

When he turns back to me, it's with the same flat expression as before, with only a slight glimmer in his eyes.

He gestures at the narrow hallway at the side of the room. It leads to two tiny bedrooms side by side. "Go to sleep," Hansel says. "We'll talk in the morning."

2
GRETEL

J don't expect to fall asleep quickly, or
even at all. But I climb into the narrow
bed Hansel offered me, pull the worn blanket around
my shoulders, and I'm dreaming within seconds.

I dream of the summer, as it was before everything fell apart. Soft, green grass under my bare feet.
The stream running through the forest. Market days
in the village that went late into the long summer
nights.

I dream of dancing by the bonfire in the town
square at midsummer and walking home with
Hansel, laughing. Our feet ached so badly he had to
pick me up and carry me the last stretch, but I
would've kept dancing if he wanted to.

We were only children. We knew not what was coming.

I dream of birds singing in the morning and rain falling on the roof at night and the sound of people laughing at the tavern in the distance.

That was what our village *used* to sound like. It doesn't anymore. The fog has driven people inside, and they only come out when they absolutely must. The bitter cold doesn't help.

But in my dream, it's warm and sunny, and everything looks how it should. The fog hasn't taken over the village. The fields haven't burned. There hasn't been a famine.

Hansel still smiles at me. I can't make out most of what he's saying, but just from his expression, I think he's talking to me about taffy.

He always wanted taffy.

We must agree to go get some, because at some point in the dream I turn around and find him eating a piece. He offers me some, and it's sweet. I haven't tasted sweets like this in so long.

In the dream, I close my eyes and savor it.

I don't know when it ends. I don't know if it does.

When I wake up, I think I'm still there. For a

moment there is peace and hope. It's been so long since I've felt that.

Still in the summer I dreamed of. I'm warm under the covers, and the pillow is soft under my head, and it smells like Hansel's cottage. I can't remember why I'm sleeping here. Did I run here for shelter from a storm? Did we stay up too late talking?

My heart sinks as the memories of last night come back to me. One by one, the memories school me.

It wasn't a late-night conversation or a summer storm that brought me here. It was the witch. Her curse and our torment.

I'm in this bed, in Hansel's house, because I forced myself out of my house and to his doorstep. I came inside and looked him in the face while he glared at me. I told him about the rocks leading to my house, and the rocks in my living room, and how I *know* she's back.

We'll talk in the morning, Hansel said.

I keep my eyes squeezed shut. The mattress might be thin and hard, and the blanket is threadbare in places, but I'm warm and safe for the moment, and I don't want the moment to end.

I give myself to the count of five, breathing slow

and pretending I'm still asleep, then get up and wash my face in the little basin in the corner. It's freezing outside the bed. The heat from the fire doesn't reach into the tiny bedrooms, and if it did, it would be a waste of firewood. I was warm enough while I slept.

Once I've dried my face, I tug the blanket off the bed and wrap it around my shoulders. It's early, but I can hear movement in the kitchen.

I take a deep breath and leave the tiny bedroom. It's right next to the slightly bigger room where Hansel sleeps. I peek in and find the blanket made up. It doesn't look slept in. I didn't hear him get in bed before I fell asleep.

The only thing that makes it easier to go to the main room is that the fireplace is there, and it will be warmer. I've been craving heat, like everyone else in town, so I square my shoulders and go, my thick winter socks almost silent on the floor.

Hansel's in the kitchen. One look at him tells me he hasn't slept. There are dark circles under his eyes, and he's wearing a burdened expression along with yesterday's clothes. He's got his coat on, and his back is to me. The fire crackles in the hearth, throwing off as much heat and light as when I went to sleep.

There's a bag hanging on the hook by my cloak and *my* bag.

Hansel has already packed.

Hope springs in my chest. I can't go back alone. It was torture the last time and I don't know what waits for me. But she haunts me. I have to go and see this to the end.

I pray he comes with me and seeing the bag offers me hope.

I want to hide under the blanket. I want to disappear, just like I wanted to disappear yesterday. But I can't go back now. I need to be certain Hansel understands that what's happening is real.

I wrap the blanket tighter around my shoulders, my chest clenching, and pad across to the kitchen table.

Hansel cracks an egg into a pan on the stove, then glances over his shoulder at me. He lifts his chin in a quick acknowledgment, but doesn't say a word.

It's been years since I've spoken to him in confidence. After what happened, when we came home, there was concern that drifted us apart.

We have to talk, but I can't say I'm in a hurry to start the conversation. The quiet used to be comfortable between us. Now a thick tension hangs in the air and makes my throat ache. The last thing I want to do is talk about the past, or the witch, or the stones, so I sit there in silence while Hansel cooks.

I can't help looking at him.

He's taller than he was when we were younger. His shoulders are broader. He's on the slim side, but then—everyone in the village is. That's what happens when there's a famine, and a wildfire, and when most of us are on the edge of starving.

I wish I could get close to him, even if it was just under the pretense of staying warm. I want to go to him and put my arms around his waist and let my nose brush the back of his jacket. He was the only friend I had. And when we parted, I had no one. And neither did he. No one could understand what we'd been through. But everyone thought it wise to keep us apart. I could press a kiss to his back so lightly he wouldn't notice. I could simply *feel* him—his sturdy muscles and his strong heartbeat.

I could feel his warmth.

Readjusting the blanket, I sit quietly and press my thighs together under the table. My whole body screams to get up and go to him. My body doesn't care that Hansel hates me. It just wants him, in every way there is to want someone. I can't *stop* wanting him. It doesn't matter that he doesn't want me anymore.

Not as a friend and not as anything more.

He's always had a hold on me, like something out of a fairytale. It was Hansel I dreamed about at night. When I was younger, my dreams were sweet. Taffy and holding hands and smirking at one another.

When I got older, and Hansel got tall and handsome, my dreams got less sweet and more... sinful. I dreamed about his body under his clothes and his hair wet from swimming in the river and how his mouth would feel on mine. The childish love I felt for him became something hot and irresistible. I learned what a craving was because that was the only word I could find to describe how I wanted him. *Needed* him.

To take away what was and protect me again like he once did.

I shake my head and pull the blanket as tight around me as I can. I didn't come here because I'd hoped there was still hope for us.

Hope abandoned us long ago.

The rocks. The *witch*.

Thinking of her, even for a few seconds, turns my blood to ice. I focus back on watching Hansel cook.

His hands are large—a man's hands—but capable as he cooks the eggs and warms the bread in the pan the way I used to love when we were kids. Hansel adds a few sausages to the pan as well, which makes my heart twist all over again.

Food is hard to come by in the village. What little there is costs more than it ever has before. Hansel and his father don't have much—nobody does—and yet he's going to offer some of it to me.

The aroma of the breakfast fills the cabin. Hansel takes down three plates from an open shelf near the stove and puts food on one of them. My mouth waters as he carries it to the table and puts it down in front of me, along with a fork and a folded napkin made from cloth that used to be the color of a robin's egg and is closer to gray now.

I look up to thank him and find his eyes burning into mine. His eyes are still so beautiful, and so *angry*, that I can't say a word.

"We're going to find that house," he says, his voice soft. "And I'm going to burn it down. I'll show you there's no witch. She's dead."

The bitterness in his words is at odds with the warmth of the plate.

He's wrong. She's not dead, and she's been trying to lure me back. The determination in Hansel's expression steals my words. He doesn't understand. He never has. I wish he were right though. We killed her and I wish she'd stay dead. The horrors are too much and we were only children.

"I—" I swallow thickly, struggling to breathe and get my thoughts in order. *I want you to be the person you were.* I can't say that to Hansel. Not when it's my fault he's like this. *I'm glad you're angry.* No. I'm not glad he's angry. I'm not glad *any* of this happened. But he looks fierce and full of life, and he used to look like that when we were kids. Only he was fierce about me, and not *this*. Meekly, I admit, with the only words I can find, "I don't remember how to get there."

Hansel's eyes narrow a little more. "I do."

"I wouldn't have thought you—"

"I've been back before."

My heart jolts with surprise. He's been *back*? I had no idea he went to the witch's cottage without me. I honestly didn't think he ever would—even if I were with him. My hands ache around the fabric of the blanket.

My lips part with shock, but I can't think of a word to say.

Hansel turns his back to me. I fist my hands around the fabric of the blanket to stop myself from reaching for him. I have so many questions. *When* did he go back? What was it that made him go? Is that why he's so sure the witch is still dead?

Maybe he's right. Maybe the long winter has simply made me go mad.

How long did he spend wondering about her before he went?

I don't know how to ask Hansel anymore.

The bedroom door opens behind me, and I stand up, going automatically towards the sound.

"Good morning," I say quietly, offering my arm as I reach for him, Hansel's father.

"Gretel," he says, and takes my arm. I can tell he wishes he didn't need my help, but doesn't want to spare the energy to say so. He leans on me until we get to the table, then sits down in one of the seats next to mine. He's always been kind. If only life was as kind to him as he deserved.

Hansel brings the other two plates. He sets one in front of his father, and one at the spot across from me, then sits.

"Father," he says. "Mary from next door is coming to stay for a few days. I have somewhere I need to go."

Hansel's father takes this in and gives Hansel a solemn nod, sadness in his eyes but no surprise on his face. He knows what happened. He wept when we returned. I can only imagine what went through the widower's mind when we were gone. The poor man. Life is cruel and it spared him none.

"You have everything you need?" he questions quietly.

"Yes," Hansel answers. "We'll leave after we eat."

He picks up his fork and slices one of his sausages in two. Hansel's father and I follow his lead. I bow my head and concentrate on my breakfast. It's simple food, and it smells delicious. It's been a long time since anyone cooked a meal for me, and I find myself wanting to memorize it.

In case I don't come back.

And because Hansel hasn't willingly given me even so much as a smile in so long that it makes these eggs and these slices of toast and these sausages precious beyond the worth they hold when food is so scarce.

We eat without speaking. It's almost possible to pretend that we're just slow to wake up and enjoying a comfortable quiet breakfast together and not swallowing our own heartbreak…or hate, in Hansel's case.

He's cooked the eggs just as I like—on the fluffy side—and he clearly made the bread himself. There's not much to go around, but it's hearty. The sausage is spicy and gone too soon.

Hansel finishes first. I'm not far behind. When I move to get up and collect the plates, Hansel jumps to his feet and stacks them first, then strides determinedly to the sink. He lets them drop into it with a loud *thunk* and grabs a scrub-brush from a hook on the wall. There's practically nothing to sweep up—none of us wanted to waste a crumb—but I grab the broom from its corner and slide it across all the floors.

I've just put it back in its place—and Hansel's putting the last plate on the rack to dry—when there's a knock at the door.

Hansel doesn't glance at me. He goes to the door and opens it.

"Mary," he says, and bends down to give Mary a hug.

"Hansel," she says warmly, patting his back, and then she spies me over his shoulder. Her eyebrows shoot up toward the sky. "Gretel!"

Mary's a petite, kind-faced woman who bustles in and puts her arms around me without hesitating. I have to swallow a lump in my throat as I hug her back. The village blames me for what happened. Nobody will say it to my face, but I know they're all thinking it—and honestly, I agree with them. Things could have been so different for all of us. I was the one who begged him to come with me. I needed to see if there was anything out there. I regret it and the town regrets my existence.

But Mary pushes me a step back and looks me up and down. "You look well," she proclaims, and pats my face. "I hope you're not intending to be gone long. You're not, are you?"

"No, I'm not planning to be gone long," I tell her, and let go. Her shawl covers most of her; the older woman's gray hair is braided beneath the cloth.

She heads to the table next and helps Hansel's father up from his chair. The two of them go across to the fire, and Mary settles him in, tucking a blanket over his lap and fussing over him. They've both suffered loss and in each other's company they can be alone together.

They're not *gone,* but they're far enough away that it feels like Hansel and I are alone in the kitchen.

His eyes are dark with emotion as he crosses his arms over his chest. "You'll need to change," he says. "I'll prepare the horse and the wagon. We'll go as soon as you're ready."

Don't you want to talk first? I bite back the question. "I won't take long."

He nods, his jaw clenching, and looks away.

I hurry to the hooks by the door and get my bag, then hurry to the narrow bedroom. I don't have much to change into. A warmer underdress. A wool sweater. My thickest socks.

I smooth out the sheets on the bed and tuck the blanket back in.

When I emerge a few minutes later, Hansel's waiting by the door with his bag slung over his shoulder. Mary and Hansel's father are with him. Hansel's father pats Hansel's shoulder.

I go to join them, my heart heavy. I don't want to take Hansel from his father. I can't do this without him. I wish none of this had ever happened. I can't escape the fact that it did.

Selfishness comes over me and I nearly change my mind. But she has to die, once and for all. I need to make sure the witch is dead.

Hansel gives his father one last goodbye and heads out the door. Mary embraces me. Hansel's father squeezes my shoulder as I move toward the door.

"Take care of my boy," he says softly, then closes the door behind us.

3

HANSEL

*T*he fog is so thick I can hardly see Gretel at the doorstep. She's mostly a shadow, looking smaller, somehow, than she used to look. Not that Gretel was ever tall. But she used to stand up straighter. She didn't look so afraid. We were only kids and life hasn't been kind to either of us. Her timid nature is evidence of that.

I feel for her. She's fucking terrified and I haven't seen her like that since... The memories assault me and I'm taken back there, for only a moment before I shut it down. The witch is dead. We aren't children anymore. And she needs to know it's over.

If only it was a nightmare, one I've spent years attempting to wake from.

As I watch her stare off down the road as if the

witch is waiting for us, all of the feelings I've spent years suppressing rage inside of me.

Last time I let my feelings get the better of me, we ended up in that witch's house, and it ruined our lives. *Not just ours.*

I bristle at the thought.

I've already got the wagon ready. The horse is harnessed. I spent half of the night awake, thinking of Gretel in the next room, tossing and turning like the teenager I used to be.

I'm not that boy anymore. And she's not that girl who longed for laughter and adventure. Life didn't want her spirit so bright.

"Ready?" I call, hating that this is what brought us together again.

"Yes," she answers, though just from her tone, I can tell she doesn't want to do this. She's already having regrets.

Gretel needs to know she's wrong. She needs to understand that we killed that witch, and the fog has nothing to do with us. This curse is steadfast but it doesn't' mean the witch lives. She burned in that oven. Her stench ever present if only I think of the dreadful day. The scream... it haunts me and I imagine it haunts Gretel as well.

Gretel comes to me, her steps tentative, and I

hold out my hand to aid her into the wagon. The wood is old and creaks, but it will keep us warm for the journey. It's hard to imagine we went by foot as children. I've taken the path so many times since, from hatred and fueled by pain. My chest is hollow as I think of going one last time. One last time and this time, I'll burn that whole house down.

And what would that mean for the two of us?

Gretel glances up at me, then puts her hand in mine. I force myself not to make a sound. Her hands are just as delicate as I remember, but strong, too. I want to hold her hand. I want to hold it like we did so many times before.

I don't. I boost her up onto the step and steady her while she climbs over and sits on the bench seat.

"Hup," I say, my voice carrying out in the fog as I lift the reins. The horse hears, and trots forward.

The wooden wheels are loud on the street, which is part cobblestone, part dirt. I feel every jolt as we bump away from my father's house. The clatter of the wheels echoes in my ears.

I try to stare straight ahead; I can't help but to search the fog for any sign of movement. Each heartbeat of mine is heavy and thumps loudly in my ears. It's hard to see anything but the outlines of buildings and hints of doors and windows. Once or twice, I see someone's shadow in a window, but that could be a trick of the light. It's early morning and we've got a long way to go. So far silence is our only company.

Gretel says nothing as we leave the village. The cobblestones give way to dirt, and the sound of the wheels doesn't rattle back at us anymore. It disappears into the fog.

Thin snowflakes spiral down from a sky we can't see. It's probably as white as the fog, and just as chilling. I blink a few flakes out of my eyes. They're sharp. Not like the fluffy snowdrifts of my childhood at all.

I wanted to go out in it, then. I wanted to make snowballs and build a snowman and catch the snow on my tongue. I wanted to chase Gretel and watch her cheeks go pink.

Now all I want is to be *inside*. Warm by a fire. Safe.

Alone. Not chasing demons I've long since killed.

The cold and the silence are worse with Gretel sitting at my side.

I try to tell myself I don't care, but I do.

This isn't how our last time together should be.

This *is* our last time together. I swallow thickly at the thought.

Once we return to the village, she'll leave me once again. She can go back to whatever life it is she's made for herself and leave me out of it.

It shouldn't hurt so much to imagine that. It's not as if I asked her to come here. But out here, in the oppressive fog and the bitter cold, it makes my heart ache like I just lost her all over again. For a moment, a small moment, I want to ask her to not leave so quickly this time. Just stay a moment.

It's the memories that make it hardest of all. We could always talk before. If we ran out of things to do, we could lie on our backs on a hill and watch the clouds roll overhead for hours, talking about whatever crossed our minds. I could always think of something new to tell Gretel, or ask her, or wonder about with her.

The farther we get from town, the colder it gets, and the more my heart aches. It's going to be a long day if it hurts more like this with every mile.

We bump along behind my horse. My hands are cold in the gloves, which need to be thin so I can work the reins.

I'm surprised when Gretel inches toward me on the bench.

I don't mean to stiffen at her touch, but I do. She

lets out a short breath, like she's disappointed, but doesn't move away.

Maybe she just needs a scrap of human comfort and warmth. The thought settles something in my chest although I can't place it.

I'm the only one here to give her warmth. It doesn't mean anything that she's come closer. She's only here to make sure the witch is dead. She didn't come back for me. And why would she? When surely I remind her of what happened... I know she reminds me of–

"Is the fog getting thicker?" she asks, cutting off my thoughts.

"I can't tell," I answer bluntly and she shifts slightly. I nearly second guess myself.

It's better than silence. I feel like I'm holding my words in my fists. I can't loosen them. They're practically frozen and my movements paralyzed.

For a while afterwards, I try to figure out whether the fog *is* getting thicker ahead of us. Is it warning us away, or trying to entice us into a mystery?

Or is it doing nothing of the kind, because it's only fog?

It's only fog. Gretel will see.

She stays close as we go. When she's touching me, even through all our layers and on this hopeless trip, it makes it easier to breathe. Her weight is gentle against my side and I find myself wanting more. Needing more of her leaning against me. Wanting me to provide for her.

With nothing much to look at in the fog, my mind begins to wander.

Back to that night.

Back to the witch's house.

Back to everything that happened there.

"There will be an answer in the house," Gretel says softly. "I know it."

I make a sound in the back of his throat. The memories feel like a hard lump. "That's what the witch said." *We will answer for what we did to her.*

"That's not all she said," Gretel reminds me, her voice low and full of fear.

"I know."

I've thought of it so many times. She cast that spell before her last breath.

I think of the witch again when Gretel's elbow presses a little harder against mine. I don't have to do much to guide the horse around what must be a curve in the road, but I lean into Gretel anyway, letting the touch grow warmer. I wish I could wrap my arm around her and comfort her as if the spell was being cast now.

The witch's words repeat in my mind. I've never been able to forget them.

THE MOST POWERFUL *of magic will claim you both, you'll see.*

You cannot escape what is destined, so mote it be.

FOR DAYS AND WEEKS, the witch's threat left me with dread. But it faded with time as I grew older. There was only the witch.

She wanted to scare us. Ruin our lives. Fill us with fear as her final dying wish.

I shake my head, letting out a low scowl.

"What is it?" Gretel asks.

"Nothing," I say.

How am I supposed to tell her that I can't get that night out of my head? That I dream about it all the time? That all I want to do is forget? The curse might not be real, but what happened to us is very real.

A shape appears in the fog.

"Look," I say, grateful for a distraction.

Gretel looks in the direction I nod to. The shadowy figures of the old barns are barely visible in the fog. She swallows hard, knowing as well as I do that those are the last buildings on the outskirts of the village. Passing them feels like a point of no return.

We can turn back, I remind myself. *We can always go home again.*

Except there is no home. Not the way it used to be. Not since everything happened.

"The fires." Gretel moves even closer as she speaks. I don't want to talk about the destruction that came to our village, but she steels herself. "She made them happen."

"She was dead." The witch didn't do those things. It was bad luck. I lean forward a little, trying to see through the fog. Doesn't help.

Gretel looks ahead, too.

I can see my horse's mane, but not much farther. My whole body is sore from how tense I was all night. I wanted to go to her, even if it wouldn't fix anything.

"How do you explain them, then?" Gretel asks. "All the bad things that happened to our town."

So *much* happened.

When we got back from the witch's cottage, we told everyone who would listen. At first we were met with skepticism but when we cried and showed the scars and brought them back to the house, fear spread like the wildfire would.

The next night, alone and scared, I knocked on her door. I was broken, still hurt, and all I could think to do was grab her hand, pull her to me and kiss her. I could taste the salt of her dried tears. I promised myself, if we stayed together, we could protect each other from the terrors of what happened.

I put my arms around her under the full moon and I let myself do something I'd never done before. I kissed her and she kissed me back. With a desperation to forget the pain and simply be loved by someone who knew every piece of you and still loved you.

But right then the door opened, and her father was standing there with bags slung over his shoulders and a look on his face that didn't mean anything good.

"We're leaving," he barked. "See yourself home, Hansel." He shoved me back, whatever moment was there, was broken.

"Father," Gretel protested. "It's dark. We can't—"

"We're leaving," he repeated, his voice stern but also full of dread, and shifted the bag to his other arm so he could pull Gretel along with him. The tale of what we went through had spread through the town and fear was potent. It drifted from her father as he rushed them away.

I followed them, numb. He already had their horse harnessed to their small, rickety wagon and more belongings packed inside. They didn't have much to begin with, but seeing it all piled in the wagon like that made my stomach clench.

"Where are you taking her?" I questioned and he ignored me. The man was already gone by the looks in his eyes.

"Hansel," she cried out as she looked back, her eyes shining, but her father steered her into the wagon.

And then she was gone. Stolen away in the middle of the night. Taken from me.

The very next week, the fires came.

I don't know how Gretel's father heard about the fires. Everyone must have known. I didn't know he had come back to help fight them until someone found his body.

He was pinned down at the far corner of one of the fields when the flames backed him into a wooden storage shed meant to hold tools for the harvest. All the work we did fighting the fires came to nothing. They burned too hot, and too fast. The whole village together couldn't stop them.

When the sun came up, Gretel was an orphan.

Nobody could tell me what happened to her.

Weeks past and I suffered alone, some doubting what happened, others fearing what I would bring next. They blamed me, some even hated me. I stopped trying to find her.

I was drowning in the pain from the witch's cottage. Sometimes I'd hear rumors about how she was with this relative, or that one. This village or that one. But she didn't send a letter. I didn't hear from her.

I started to think maybe she blamed me too. Maybe she hated me too.

The only other time I saw her was when she came back to her father's old house, which had sat empty after she left.

By then it was too late. I was bitter, and felt betrayed, and I wanted nothing to do with her. The famine had already hit hard. It was a struggle to find work. And a very deep part of me didn't want her to stay. Not when this life was waiting for her. She had a chance to run. If only I could run with her.

I didn't recognize myself anymore. Gretel didn't seem to recognize the person I'd become, either.

"Let's play a game," she blurts out, as if she's been thinking the same thing and decided those memories are too painful for right now. "Never have I ever." Her voice is oddly uplifting for the mood I find myself in.

My brow arches. A child's game? Silence contemplates with me before I acquiesce. "You go first, then."

"Never have I ever..." Gretel bites her lip, her brow furrowed. "Kissed someone... like other than you."

"Is that so?" I say shocked. She's lovely. Beautiful in every way. How could someone not take her hand as I did?

"I've forgotten what it even feels like," she whispers, her eyes wide and staring deep into mine. A fire blazes within me.

"Gretel," I warn, my voice low. "You know not what you do."

She stares at me a moment and although I try to look away, I'm caught in her gaze.

"I know what I'm doing. I miss you."

I pull on the reins, and my horse clatters to a stop. I reach for her without hesitation, put my hand on her face, and pull her in for a kiss.

Her lips mold to mine, just like it used to be, and she opens for me, letting me explore her in a deep, hot kiss.

I'm greedy for it. Feels like fire to kiss her. Like every piece of me is being awakened for the first time since we got back from the witch's house.

She moans into my mouth and I feel the sweet sound everywhere. It's far too much and the lusty haze clears for a moment.

I pull back to catch my breath. I grip her chin for a few more beats before I can force myself to let go.

"There," I say, my heart racing, and take the reins again, urging the horse on.

There's silence, after that. Every thought races in my mind. I don't have an answer to any question and I have no idea if she feels what I feel. If this racing in my blood is what fuels her teasing me.

"Well?" I say.

"Well?" Gretel repeats.

"Is it my turn?"

"I don't—" Gretel shakes her head. "I don't think..."

"Alright."

We roll along down the road for a while. The quiet now doesn't seem as strained as it did before. Maybe I'm just imagining that, but I hope I'm not.

"Did you want to play it just to kiss me?" I ask her.

She hesitates but then answers, "Not at first. I just wanted to talk."

I nod, believing her and then let my breath turn to fog in front of my face.

"You look the same," I can't help saying. It's the first thing I thought of when she came back to town, and it's the first thing I thought of when I opened the door for her last night.,

"What?"

"You look the same." I nudge her elbow with mine. "But older."

Gretel huffs a laugh. "Well, that's good, I suppose. How much older?"

I laugh, then. It's the first real laugh I think I've laughed in months. Maybe even years. It reminds me of what we used to be. "You look good, Gretel. You taste good too."

She turns her face away, probably to hide that she's blushing. There's so much more I want to say, but none of it makes any sense. It's all nonsense about how I felt about her. How I missed her. How I don't understand how she could leave me when I needed her so. How I want to know.

I can't make myself say any of it.

After a minute, I exhale and focus back on the road.

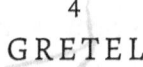

4

GRETEL

*I*t feels like we've been traveling a long time when the fog starts to fade into sky.

I try to remember how long it took before, but I quickly put an end to the memories. I don't necessarily trust my memories of that time and even the good parts have soured over time.

The fog doesn't completely disappear, but it settles into more of a fine mist than the thick, choking fog surrounding the village and everywhere around it. Above us, the sky is a wintery grey. It's not exactly sun bursting through the clouds, but even that grey is a welcome sight after so much time hidden in the fog.

It doesn't take long though for the open fields to be lost to a forest of black, leafless trees. The branches block out a lot of the light. And so we move through the forest in the evening shadows.

This time, I don't try to be casual about getting closer to Hansel.

He wanted to kiss me after all and his warmth is a welcome distraction. His lips on mine are more than I dreamed. And I have dreamed of him so many nights. I needed to just to fall asleep and keep the demons of the past away. I can still feel the warmth of his touch even as we're surrounded by the coldest winter.

The shadows on either side of the path are unnerving and seem to move in ways they shouldn't. This part of the forest does *not* look friendly, and I can't imagine how we ignored it when we were younger.

The answer is that we didn't. We saw them, and we were scared, and we kept going, because—

I shiver and pull my cloak tighter around me. My left side pressed against Hansel as I huddle under the cloak. Everything is warm enough but the tip of my nose and my toes. But the bits of me that press against Hansel feel safest of all.

The path leads us deeper and deeper into the forest.

Hansel urges his horse down a branching path,

and then another. It's a good thing he's here. I don't remember taking these paths before. They all look the same to me.

But then Hansel calls the horse to a halt.

The horse stops beside a gap in the trees.

Hansel hops down, but I stay frozen on the bench seat until he comes around and offers me his hand.

"It's fine, Gretel," he says, but the look in his eyes says it's not.

"Promise?" I whisper and he nods, "I promise."

I'm the one who asked him to come here. So I take his hand and hop down.

My shoe sends a small pebble flying off the path. There's not much snow beneath the branches, but the pebble disappears into it.

Back then, we left stones along the path we took so we could find our way out. They were the same sorts of stones that have been appearing outside my house now. White quarts with a crystalline shine. They looked so pretty in the light back then. But now all I see is the sharpness of the stones.

Hansel curls his hand around mine, keeping the reins in the other, and leads Cinnamon through the gap in the trees.

At the sight of the shelter, my heart races. My blood goes cold. I can barely breathe.

The witch's cottage is in the middle of a little clearing. It's a small, wooden cottage with a peaked roof, all of it deep brown, like tree bark. I can't see in the front windows. They're too dark.

It looks...lonely. Almost abandoned.

Hansel ties his horse up to a post in a small, covered area attached to the house, but takes the harness off and rubs him down a bit with gloved hands. There's a trough on the other side filled with melted snow, and from a covered wooden box, he grabs dried straw. Hansel rummages around in a wooden trunk nestled next to the house and comes up with a thick blanket, which he puts over the horse's back. It's almost like he's been here before. Like the cottage was prepared for him. Although my feet are firmly planted, I feel the need to run. Fear tramples through me.

The horse, though, is calm. He eats the straw without worry. Huddled under a roof and seemingly content with its shelter.

Hansel must think his horse will be fine here, because he pulls off his gloves and bends down to scoop some snow off the ground. Hansel uses it to clean his hands, then pats them dry on his shirt. He tucks his gloves into one of his pockets. With a nod, he gestures for me to follow and although it's difficult, I move one foot after the other.

"How did you find it?" I ask Hansel as we approach the cottage. "When you first went back." His knuckles brush against my hand. I'm quick to hold it. Our fingers thread between one another. Each step brings me closer and closer to a place that holds such horrors.

He squeezes my hand. "It took a while." The pain in those simple words brings on memories I've tried my hardest to avoid since we came back.

I haven't forgotten anything. Not a single thing, other than the way to get here.

The witch's face, terrifyingly happy to have us there with her. The stew that bubbled in a huge cauldron over the fire. The sound of Hansel's muffled gasps. The way the screams felt as they ripped themselves out of my throat. How heavy the chains were around my wrists.

I swallow hard, my stomach turning. My skin prickles with goosebumps. The witch was a monster, and she was nothing like the scary stories my father told when I was young.

She was *real.*

I pull on Hansel's hand until he stops, mere feet from the door.

"Hansel." My mouth is sticky with fear. "Maybe I was wrong. Maybe we shouldn't—"

His hand tightens on mine and he presses his lips into a thin line. "We're going in, Gretel. You need to see that she's not here. There's no one here."

I don't want to. I *never* want to go into that cottage again. But I don't think the witch is dead, and if Hansel's right—

I need to know if he's right, or if I am. I need to know how to fix this.

Hansel tries the door.

It must not be barred from the inside, because it swings open with ease. All the while my blood rushes in my ear. There's a small scream in the back of my head begging me to stop. To not go back. He drops my hand when I don't move. Paralyzed by fear.

"Dark in there," Hansel says, and steps forward, holding the door open with his shoulder and peeking in. "Doesn't seem like anyone's here. Come on."

I glance back at the horse. We have a way out this time. We have a horse and a wagon. We're older now. We're not trapped. *She's dead.* I repeat the truth, she's dead. She can't hurt us anymore.

I take a deep breath and let Hansel lead me inside.

I jump when the door thumps shut behind us, whirling toward it. But it's only Hansel.

He pats the door with the palm of his hand. His blue eyes shine with sincerity as he waits for my heart to calm

"Just me," he says. "Now we won't freeze while we're looking around." His lips lift slightly as if offering a smile but it falls short. His stubble is rough, his skin thicker and it's only now that I realize just how handsome a man Hansel's become.

I would rather keep the door open, even if it means we freeze, but Hansel's right. We should do our best to stay warm. He turns the latch and tugs on it, testing its strength.

It doesn't come apart in his hand, so I hope it can keep the door closed to any intruders. As if there's anyone else so far deep in the wild woods.

The main room of the cottage is as it was—dim and dusty. It's surprisingly neat in comparison to my memories. We didn't make a mess, but we went through a nightmare, and I expected the cottage to match the despair I felt. But it's quaint. It's not exactly how I remember although small bits of it reflect my memory.

A woven rug that used to be brightly colored squats in front of the fire. One of the wooden chairs is turned over by the table, which is one of the only signs that something horrible happened here.

The table itself is bare, except for one metal plate. A few other dishes line a shelf over the sink. Dried herbs hang from hooks by the window. Nothing looks like it's been touched in a long, long time.

It certainly doesn't look like anyone's living here right now.

But my skin is still covered in goosebumps. I can't help the chill just being in this place.

I don't trust my own eyes. I don't trust the emptiness here. It reminds me of the fog, somehow, only I can't put my finger on why. Maybe it's just another reminder of the pain I caused. It's pain that's followed us to this day.

I brace myself and turn towards the last object in the main room, the big iron oven. My heart thuds in my ears. If the witch pushes open the oven door and crawls out, the image flashes in front of my eyes and a scream tries to claw up my throat. But it's not real. The oven is still. The reality is that this place is empty. Still, I'm slow to move. Terrified that the nightmares are real.

It's dark as the windows, no fire lit inside, but the sight of it makes me want to be sick.

Hansel holds my hand tighter and pulls me with him to the oven. He doesn't release my hand when he bends down and opens the thick door on the front. It creaks on its hinges like it hasn't been opened since.

"Come look, Gretel."

"I don't want to."

"Come look," he urges. "I'm here. Right beside you and there's nothing to be afraid of."

I hesitate until he adds, "I promise."

Slowly, and cautiously, I bend down next to him.

The oven is empty. There's nothing inside. Not even the ash.

There's no sign of her at all. Just an old oven, in an old cottage. No proof of any wickedness at all. Because she's gone. She's dead.

Relief slowly spreads through me, although I still don't quite trust it. Foolishness runs through me. Embarrassment almost. Of course she's dead. She's long since perished. The stones… perhaps I imagined them. I don't know anymore. Perhaps I've gone crazy with fear.

"It's empty," he says firmly, then straightens up. Hansel drops my hand and brushes them on his pants. I look up to apologize to him, but then I see his hardened expression. His furrowed brow and stern look.

He's upset. Maybe even angry. Hansel has every right to be angry at me.

We came to this house because I dared him all those years ago.

It was the kind of thing that kids from the village did. Every so often, we'd go on a long ramble, pretending we were travelers. Our legs could carry us a decent distance. But we'd never seen this cottage before.

Hansel and I made it all the way here. We had to sleep out overnight to do it without a wagon, but we didn't care. It was summer, and the stars were out. We were having an adventure.

We didn't think anything bad could happen to us.

But it *did*.

The forest looked mysterious in the summer, with all the leaves waving on the branches and the long, dark paths leading to unknown places. Every time one of us wanted to turn back, the other would make another dare.

A little farther, then a little farther, then a little farther.

When we came to the clearing and saw the

cottage, I couldn't resist. I dared Hansel to go up and knock on the door.

We hadn't expected anyone to answer.

I ran to Hansel's side when the door cracked open and took his hand.

We went inside together.

We were not the same when we came back out. As I watch the pain morph into Hansel's expression, I remember what he must be remembering. All the agony she put us through.

The witch chained me up, but she tortured Hansel. I screamed until I couldn't make a sound. I still have scars from where the metal dug into my skin.

He was different after that. He didn't want anything to do with me, and I can't blame him. How could I ever blame him? He wasn't the one who suggested knocking on the door. If I hadn't done it—

If I hadn't dared him, maybe we would have walked back out of the forest and headed home. Maybe our lives could have stayed simple.

But that's not what happened.

Something hits the floor with a loud 'bang' and brings me out of my memories. Hansel pulls pieces of wood off a stack in the corner. It's the same stack that was here the last time we were. He kicks one of the fallen logs back into place and turns to face me.

"I'll make a fire. We'll stay here tonight."

The darkness outside lets me know there's no way we'd be able to make it through the woods. "Here?" I question and he looks back at me as though it's an odd question.

"We have to rest before heading back. We've travelled all day and night."

There's no hearth in the little cottage. It's heated —when it's heated—by the oven. While Hansel tips the wood into the oven and gets the fire started, I find a broom in the opposite corner. I find a rag near the sink and use it to brush away the cobwebs from the broom, then use the broom to brush the worst of the cobwebs off the walls and corners. Then I do the floor, starting near the door and working my way around.

Hansel shuts the oven with a *clang* just as I reach the doorway. I'm simply keeping myself busy. Exhaustion weighs down on me but I don't know how I could possibly sleep here. Foolishness once again sinks it's claws into me.

The cottage has one bedroom, and I hesitate at the door.

It must have been *her* bedroom. But it was also

where she kept us, for a little while. It was where she kept me when she tortured Hansel.

Not wanting to make this any worse for Hansel, I lift my chin and go inside. One foot after the other even though my body feels frozen and unmoving.

It's as dim as the rest of the cottage, but I attack all the cobwebs and brush some of the dust off the window. Not quite looking and thinking of the fire.

I lean the broom in the corner and move to the bed. It's big enough for two people, but I want the faded blanket off. I pull it away from the mattress, fold it up, and stack it in a free corner. There's a chest at the foot of the bed, and I open it, hoping—

Yes. There's another quilt inside. I shake that one out and spread it out on the bed. All the while my heart races and my mind begs me not to think of anything. The back of my eyes sting with the memories. I can hardly breathe.

It was so awful here, and it was all my fault. Hansel shouldn't forgive me. He shouldn't touch me ever again. He was right, and I was wrong, and I've always *been* wrong, and—

"Maybe we don't need to stay," I manage, and turn to face Hansel directly behind me. "Maybe—"

He closes the distance between us and puts one

hand on my waist, the other on my chin. Hansel tilts my face to his and looks into my eyes.

He doesn't look blank anymore. He doesn't look like a stranger. He looks like the boy I knew, grown into a man and hurt badly along the way. There's so much pain in his eyes that I can't believe he's not crying.

No tears well up. He rakes his eyes over my face, his thumb tracing a path over my bottom lip.

Hansel lets out a breath. "Gretel it's okay."

"I don't think we have to stay," I whisper in a rush. *I'm* the one with tears slipping onto my cheeks, and I can't stop them. "I'm not afraid to travel at night, as long as I'm not—" I stumble over the words. "As long as I'm not alone. We shouldn't stay here. We should never have come here in the first place. We—"

"Shh." Hansel runs his thumb over my lips until I quiet. "Never have I ever—"

"Hansel, please. You don't have to—"

"Never have I ever fucked anyone in this house," he says, stealing my breath. "But I want to. I want to claim every inch of you. I want to change what this place means to me. I want you. I want this house to know the sounds you make under me. I want you to know what pleasure is."

My entire body trembles. It's cold in the bedroom—the heat from the oven hasn't had a chance to fill the cottage yet—but it's not the temperature that overwhelms me. It's Hansel's touch. Every nerve ending is lit aflame.

"I've never," I whisper. No one has ever spoken to me like that. No one's ever looked at me the way he does now. My body bows to his, with an aching need.

"I know," he says, and kisses me. Deeply and with a devotion that ignites a lust within me. A desire I've had for years.

It's slower than it was in the wagon. He tastes my mouth, exploring with his tongue, and pulls my waist closer to his.

This is the heat I've craved. *This* is what I've needed, and I've been so lonely without it. So hopeless. Every day I spent apart from Hansel was worse than the last, but his kiss chases away some of the ache.

His body is so strong against mine. He's so familiar. I have never wanted anyone like I want Hansel. I never thought I had a chance at feeling this again. I thought I'd lost him forever. I thought I'd have to spend the rest of my life wondering what it meant like to be loved by him.

I gasp, my emotions swelling up and spilling over before the reality comes back. Here? In this cottage? Where he suffered so much, and I couldn't help him? Should we really be doing this? Shouldn't we be *running* back to the village, where everything is ruined but at least we can sit by the fire together?

"Gretel," he says my name and I only stare back at him, wanting nothing more than to lose myself in his touch. "Kiss me," he orders. "Kiss me and forget all about it."

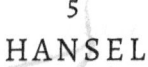

5
HANSEL

I want to forget, too.

I want to replace every memory I have in this cottage with memories of Gretel. *Only* Gretel.

I want to forget about the witch, and what she did to us. I want to burn those memories in the oven and watch them turn to ash.

Fuck that. I don't even want to think of it. I want every thought to disappear. And in its place, her. Her curves. The sweet soft sounds she makes. And the look in her eyes. That beautiful hazel longing. I want to remember that forever. Everything else can spend eternity in a hell I no longer remember.

She tips her face up to mine, making a soft moan as I kiss her deeper.

God, she's sweet. Sweeter than any candy I've ever craved. Cold air still clings to her clothes, so I run my hands up and down her sides and over her back, warming her up and loving how she shivers beneath me. It's almost too good to be true. I wish I could stay in this moment and never leave.

Gretel presses closer, her arms going around my neck. She gets up on tiptoes, her curves against my stomach, and whimpers.

"Gretel," I murmur, and push her hair away from her face. I want to *devour* her. I think I could kiss her forever if she'd let me, but there's so much *more* of her. I dip my head to lick along her neck, and Gretel gasps.

"Hansel." She tips her head back, giving me more access to the tender side of her neck, so I kiss there, too. Suck on it. The scent of her skin is intoxicating and so completely *her* that I'll never be able to tear myself away.

Not if it means giving her up.

I push that thought out of my head and angle Gretel closer. My cock is hard and in need, and she wriggles her hips slightly when she feels my hard length pressed against her, her lips parting.

Everything about her is an invitation. Her large, dark eyes. Her plush lips. The pink in her cheeks from the cold. Need surges through me like the fires surged across the fields, and suddenly I can't stand it anymore. I've been sitting next to her all day, and I need to give her something *other* than cold and fear and thinking about the witch.

"Let's get these off. They're keeping you cold."

Taking my time, I help her undress.

"Yes," she whispers, and lets me lift her dress over her head. Her underdress. I need her naked. I need to see all of her.

And then she helps me all the same. Her fingers brushing against my skin is electric. Everything about her turns me on.

I take her face in my hands. "All I care about is you."

Kissing her naked is like nothing else. I can't stop touching her. I run my hands over her hips, and her lower back, and her breasts. Leaving open mouthed kisses down the dip in her throat. I'm obsessed with every detail of her.

Gretel moans when I circle her nipple, so I stop and pay attention to both of them. God, she's so soft. She's everything I've ever wanted.

Her eyes fly open when I start to delve my hand lower.

She pants, the firelight reflecting in her eyes, and leans into me.

Then slowly, tentatively, she spreads her thighs.

"I need to touch you," I tell her.

"Yes," she breathes, and I brush my fingers between her legs.

Gretel is already wet, and so soft I could come right then and there. I take my time getting to know her. Gretel moans *oh* and *yes* and grips my arm, holding on tight while I test her opening with my fingertip.

"More," I say out loud, and pick her up in my arms.

I kiss her on the way to the bed, then lay her down on the quilt she put out. Gretel kisses me back just as hard. As if she missed me just as much as I missed her.

When I can stand to leave her mouth, I kiss down to her neck, then to her nipples, and then to her belly. Gretel's hands find my hair. Even her breathing turns me on. The arch of her back into the quilt is perfect.

I move my shoulders between her thighs and lick her clit. She's sweet as fuck and the way her hips buck at the sensation fuels me on.

Gretel lets out a long moan and opens her legs wider for me.

This is what she deserves. Everything I can give her. I lick her and taste her and swirl my tongue over her clit and lap up her arousal. I don't care about my own throbbing cock. All I care about is Gretel's pleasure, and the strangled cries of pleasure she keeps letting out, and the way her hands grab at my hair to keep my face buried in her pussy.

I suck at her clit until her thighs shake.

"Hansel," she cries out my name, her voice high and breathy. "Hansel—I'm—oh, I have to—" I don't stop, I don't let up as she thrusts herself closer and her fists ball the blanket on either side of her.

"I'm going to come," she cries out, her nipples pebbled and her back arched as pride flows through me.

Her orgasm seems to last and last, and I hold her by her hips and ride it out with her, nibbling and teasing and loving that I got her off.

And then I can't get enough of it. The second she starts to come down, I delve between her legs again and lick her until she cries out a second time and pulls me up to her, shaking.

"Please," she begs me. "Please."

"Please what?" I ask her in a murmur.

"I need you," she whispers.

Fuck, that's all I ever wanted to hear.

I've wanted to run my hands through her hair like this for years. Kiss her neck like this for years. Feel her pulse pounding from the orgasms I've just given her for *years*.

It's almost too good to be real, but I push my face into the side of Gretel's neck and kiss her again. She *is* real. We're here in this godforsaken cottage because she swore the witch was back, but the witch is as dead as she was when we left this place together.

Gretel and I are alive. And I'll be damned if this place ever haunts her again.

It doesn't take her long to recover. She turns her head and kisses me, igniting another intense wave of pure need in me. I *have* to be inside her. There's no other option. I can't live another second without being inside of her.

Gretel moves against me, almost frantic, pleadingly. Every part of me has been begging for her since the second I saw her. Why didn't I realize that sooner? Why did it take so damn long?

It doesn't matter. We're here now, and the heat from the fire fills the room, and Gretel keeps her arms around my neck as I position myself over her.

I kiss her jaw and her chin and her lips and slip my fingers between her legs. She moans softly, spreading her thighs again as I slide one finger into her slick opening. Gretel's tight but takes my finger easily, her hips rocking into my touch.

I add another finger and curl them. She shivers, more pleasure moving through her and her pussy clenching down on my knuckles.

"I need you," she murmurs. "Hansel. I need you."

"You can have me," I answer.

"Please," she says, her eyes locked on mine. "Please, Hansel."

I line myself up with her opening and push in slowly watching as her eyes widen and her breath catches.

She feels like heaven. So wet. So tight. So *mine*. I hold my breath, forcing myself to go still, then stroke Gretel's hair out of her face.

"We'll go slow," I promise her. As much as I want to fuck her with reckless abandon. I know this is her first time.

"I don't want to," she says, and rolls her hips. My eyes close and my head drops to her chest at her revelation. She doesn't know what she does to me. She doesn't realize what she's asking for.

More of me pushes inside, and we both gasp.

It feels too good to be sinking into heat, and it takes all my energy not to lose control. I need to fuck her. I need to claim her. I need her to be mine when we walk out of here again. I need everyone to know they can't take her away from me in the middle of the night, ever again.

I don't care how delirious I sound in my head. I don't care that what I want might be impossible. I'm hooked so deep in Gretel's panting, mewling sounds as she takes me inside her that nothing could bring me back out again.

Until I bottom out and she tightens around me, her thighs wrapping tight around my waist and her heels resting on my lower back. Gretel stares into my eyes, her mouth a tiny *o*.

"That's good," I tell her, and stroke my fingers through her hair. I'm going to shake myself apart if I don't fuck her soon, but at the same time, I'd be willing to wait forever for her to be ready. "You feel so good. You feel—Gretel. You feel so damn good."

"So do you," she answers, and kisses the corner of my lips. "I—" Another strong shiver.

I pull out and thrust back in. Harder and with more force. The rocking of her body forces her breasts to bounce and I'm amazed I don't come at the sight of her gorgeous curves beneath me.

"*Yes*. Yes," Gretel gasps, her feet locking behind me.

Gretel's body grips me, sending hot pleasure through my hips. I stroke into her hard, my instincts taking over, then slow it down.

I need to slow it down, or I'm going to come, and it can't be over yet.

Not when I just got her back. Not when I need her so bad I can't stand it.

I kiss her, tasting her sweet sounds, while I thrust into her, the rhythm deep and steady. Gretel whimpers again, her pussy pulsing around my cock, and comes with another burst of slick desire.

"You're *mine*," I growl into her ear, her hips rocking frantically into mine. I lose control slightly. Fucking her like I've dreamed of. She's still coming, gripping my cock so tight I'm almost blind from how good it feels. "You're mine. I'm going to make you *mine*."

"Yes, yes, yes, Hansel—Hansel—" she murmurs, her nails raking across my shoulders. *My name.* She cries out my name as I groan in the crook of her neck.

I push her a little farther onto the bed, centering her so I can fold her knees up to her chest and fuck her with everything I have.

I can't take my eyes off her heated expression. Gretel's skin is flushed and warm in the firelight, her lids half-lowered and her mouth open so she can gasp and pant and moan. She stretches one hand over her head and grips my shoulder with the other, trying to pull herself closer even as I pin her to the bed.

I need to be able to lean down over her and kiss her while I stroke into her. I need her soft and open and crying out my name. I need her desperate beneath me and at my mercy.

That's exactly what I get.

The tension that's been building in me builds and builds until I can't feel anything else. It becomes a hot, feral pleasure. I bury myself deep inside her as I find my release when she comes again.

The fire rages in the grate, twice as bright as before. A small point of flame catches my eye, and I glance at it—

Candles. On the table near the bed. There hadn't been any candles lit when we walked in, but now they're burning. Fear strikes through me and I question my vision. I blink and it's gone. Goosebumps travel down my spine but she grips onto me. Clinging to me.

Finally, I hear my own breathing, and Gretel's. I check again and there's nothing there.

She strokes my nape with her fingertips, murmuring things to me. It takes a while before I can make out what she's saying.

"So good." Gretel's breathless. She sounds satisfied. She sounds like I gave her what she needed. "That was so good, Hansel. I wanted it to be you. It had to be you. It could never be anybody else."

I don't have it in me to say anything back, so I kiss the side of her neck and pull us toward the pillow. I only need to close my eyes for a few minutes. I just need to be with her.

That's all I need. But I open my eyes, searching for whatever it was that I saw and questioning if we are alone in this cottage. I kiss her shoulder, my eyes on the open door as she whispers something I can't hear.

6

GRETEL

*H*ansel lies beside me, his arm over my waist, for what feels like a long time. But I could stay here forever. The moment my mind wanders to tomorrow, I stop my thoughts where they are and remind myself where I am at this moment. In his embrace. Loved and cherished. I wish we could stay here forever.

I've never felt this way. Nothing in my life has ever made me feel so fulfilled. Even the ache between my legs from where Hansel took me is met with a devotion from deep within my soul. It's a good kind of pain mixed with pleasure. A feeling I could definitely get used to, if I had the chance.

I was *meant* for Hansel. Hansel was meant for me. Nothing can prove to me otherwise.

Although in the back of my mind, I wander to tomorrow. To what's to come when we have to leave.

Maybe, during our time apart, I started to believe it wasn't true. Maybe I thought it would hurt less if I gave up on a silly childhood dream. Maybe it would be better for both of us, in the long run, if we weren't meant to be. Afterall, the trauma we went through scarred us both.

I've never been so *wrong* before.

Because now, with his breathing deep and even as he drifts off, I *know* he was meant for me.

Every time he touched me, it was like discovering something I'd always craved but could never name. I wouldn't have known how to *ask* anyone else for the things Hansel gave me tonight, and I didn't have to ask for any of it.

He already knew what I needed.

He already knew *me*.

The fire burns a little lower, and I watch the light from the other room while I stare at a resting Hansel remembering what he said.

You're mine. Nobody else's. I'm going to make you mine.

It makes my heart race to think of those words, but what if he feels differently when he wakes up?

What if he sees the cottage around us and remembers the fate I led him to?

Can one night together make up for how he was tortured?

A voice in the back of my mind whispers that it can't. That a hundred nights together couldn't make up for what Hansel went through. That one day, he'll look at me the way he has for years—with resentment in his eyes.

That day isn't here yet, I remind myself. *Tomorrow* isn't even here yet. For now, he's asleep, and I'm—

I shift under the blanket, letting what happened tonight seep back into me.

I've never come so hard. There have been times, alone in my bed, that I touched myself. None of those times compare *at all* to what I felt tonight. It's almost impossible to believe that the world could be so bleak outside when Hansel made me feel so good.

I curl my toes, remembering, then relax them again.

This is the kind of feeling people wait their whole lives for. People *dream* about this. They hope someone will want them enough to overwhelm them with pleasure until it's more than they've ever experienced, and then give them more on top of it.

Gods, that was *good.*

So good. Sleep threatens to take me but I resist. I don't want to sleep and leave this moment. I find myself drifting, being dragged back in time and I protest.

The firelight is warm just to watch. There wasn't any witch in the cottage, or any ash in the oven.

Maybe…

Maybe the fire in the hearth isn't a bad thing. The village has been so long without any good magic that I started to think it had disappeared from the world. But a fire in a cold cottage, warming us up?

How could that be bad?

Another memory from that night with the witch comes back to me. What was it she said?

Come in and rest, children. Have something to eat. You must be so hungry.

She'd had something in her hands. Biscuits? Cookies, maybe? Something sweet. I got a whiff of it when we were still on her doorstep, and my mouth watered. I'm sure Hansel's did, too. He always had such a sweet tooth, and sugar has always been expensive, and—

We'd been out on an adventure for two days, and we hadn't packed enough food.

But if any witch was going to seduce us into

staying overnight in the cottage, why would she have let us linger so long? Why wouldn't she have taken revenge the moment we stepped through the door?

I freeze, going still. Fear paralyzes my lungs and I can't breathe.

The witch let us linger... is she doing that now?

Is she outside the door right now? Was she only waiting until we were unarmed and distracted?

Is she going to burn down the cottage, just like the fields burn?

I listen as hard as I can. The wind blows outside. The fire crackles in the grate. Hansel mumbles something in his sleep.

My throat goes tight, but I swallow until it's normal again. No matter what happens when the sun rises, at least I have my Hansel with me. And even if it's only for tonight...

If it's only for tonight, then I'll accept that.

We're fine for the moment. Everything is fine. The witch isn't going to burn the cottage down.

Still, I decide to stay awake for a while, just to be sure. Best if one of us keeps a lookout. At least we're not sitting in a tent, or underneath a tree. We have fire. We have walls, and a door shut tight behind us.

We have each other.

I watch the shadows from the fire on the ceiling and listen for patterns in the wind.

I don't mean to drift off.

I don't know that I've fallen asleep at first. I notice the room is dark, like the fire went out, and then everything around me takes the form of that awful night. Hansel in chains. The witch, laughing. It disappears, replaced with pure darkness, and then—

A sound. Close by.

The scream tears out of my throat before I feel the terror.

It floods through my body the next second, going *everywhere.* Every nerve ending in my body is alight, not in pleasure, in pure agony. It's a deep, horrible fear. Goosebumps pull the skin on my nape tight. The tips of my fingers ache. I push myself up in the bed. *Where am I?* I don't recognize this room, or these blankets. The fire is burned down to embers. I can't see. I can't—

"Gretel." Hansel's arm comes around me, and he gathers me close to his body. He's warm, and I huddle into his warmth, shaking. "Gretel. Wake up."

Fear grips me but Hansel holds me tighter. Sleep burns my eyes but I wake, my throat raw from screaming. It takes a moment for me to understand, it was only a nightmare.

"I'm awake," I gasp. Another scream tries to fight its way out of my mouth, but I swallow it and reach for Hansel. His chest rises and falls under my hand. I blink toward the bedroom door. "I saw—I think I saw something. I think—"

"It was just a dream." He runs his hand up and down my arm. "Nothing's here."

"No," I argue. "Maybe I didn't see anything, but there's—I heard something. Something woke me up. I wasn't dreaming."

He turns my face to his and kisses me. He's tender and sweet. And slow. His love begs my heart to slow. My hands tremble and I try to look past him but he kisses me again.

That grounds me a little. I can breathe when he's kissing me. Not very deeply, but better than I was before. My lungs work, and I inhale between kisses, hoping my heart will stop pounding.

Something woke me up. I know it. My body reacted like someone had touched me. Someone who *wasn't* Hansel.

I break the kiss and glance around the room. My vision is bleary from having fallen asleep, but there's nothing here. The broom is still in the corner. Hansel's clothes and mine remain on the floor. The bedroom door is open, but there's no figure hovering at the foot of the bed or on the floor.

We're alone, but I don't *feel* alone.

Another wave of goosebumps rolls over my arms. Hansel bends his head and kisses my shoulder. "Cold?"

"No, I just think—" I look at the doorway again. There's nobody standing there, but the shadows aren't comforting. They don't look...safe. "I think something happened. I don't know what. I want to leave."

"I don't see anyone. Nothing's different from when we got into bed. It's too dark to leave, but let me stoke the fire. That'll help."

Hansel climbs out of bed, it creaks with his weight, and for a few seconds, my mind is blank except for him. I grip the covers tight around me. How could I think about anything else when he looks like that? He's always been lean, but now his muscles are carved out from the work he's done. He's loose and relaxed as he stretches his arms over his head, slips his trousers on, then pads over to the grate and takes the poker from metal holder nearby. As he does I slip my chemise and tunic on.

When Hansel stirs the embers, the fire jumps up again, little flames catching. It grows and grows once he's turned his back. The fire is alive. There's nothing to burn and yet it dances with a heat that it shouldn't.

"Hansel..." I say, my voice small.

"Yes?"

He looks over his shoulder at me, crouched in front of the fire, and my mouth goes dry.

"Do you think—"

There's a sound in the next room—a metallic *thump*, like something's falling. My hands whip to my mouth to prevent me from screaming and my body turns to ice that no fire could melt. She's here. I know she is.

I scramble out of the bed, dragging the quilt with me, and run to Hansel. It's only a couple of steps, but he's on his feet by the time I get there, the poker held out in front of him. He puts his arm out and pushes me behind him.

"Who's there?" he shouts in the direction of the other room. "Answer me."

Nobody answers. My body trembles as I look past him. My hair feels like it's standing on end.

Hansel keeps his feet planted and his arm out, but I can feel his heart hammering. Someone's *in here*. I don't want this to be how we die. I don't want this to be another nightmare.

"Who's there?" Hansel calls again, his voice stronger and full of a danger for whoever stands there in disobedience and silence.

We killed her once, I think. We'll do it again if we have to. Although my eyes sting with the painful memories, I straighten my shoulders and wait. I'll do whatever it takes to leave with Hansel by my side.

The wind blows across the roof of the cottage. It's sturdy, unlike the thatch at Hansel's house, which regularly lets in the wind and rain. What sounds like branches tip-taps over our heads. We both look up, but the sound doesn't come again.

"Stay behind me, Gretel," Hansel orders in a murmur. "Stay close. I'm going to see what that was."

He moves cautiously toward the door. I keep the quilt tight around me, though I know a quilt won't be enough if the witch is in the next room. I don't think anything will be enough if the witch is in the next room.

Hansel pauses at the doorway, the poker in front of him, and leans across. His eyes go wide although I can't see why.

"What is it?" I ask, my voice shaking.

"Food." His tone is flat.

"What?" My heart races remembering the offering that led us to our hell before.

"It's...food."

Hansel takes another step into the next room and gestures. I stay behind him but peek out to see what he's talking about.

Two candles are lit on the table. The chair that was knocked over when we first arrived is upright and pushed in.

There are dishes on the table. Plates. Bowls. Silver goblets. A meal laid out with delicacies.

The display covers most of the available space. On my next inhale, I smell it. Roasted chicken and buttery vegetables and something warm and sweet, like cookies, or cake.

We both stand there, silent, unmoving, for a minute. My own heartbeat is the loudest sound in the room, other than the wind.

Slowly, Hansel lowers the poker. He reaches back, finds my waist, and squeezes. "Are you okay?" he questions.

In an instant, all my fear rushes back. I try to speak, but all that comes out of my mouth is a choked sound. "No," I barely get out.

Hansel turns to me and puts his hand on my face. "I'll protect you, Gretel. It's going to be fine. I need you to run with me."

His voice is oddly calm. Almost too steady. His

eyes don't look flat anymore. They look determined. Hansel's hands are steady, too. They're not shaking like mine.

He turns his head, glancing around once more.

"Show yourself!" he yells out, his voice filling the small cottage.

Nothing. Not even the wind.

Hansel catches me looking. "We can't eat it," he warns.

"I know. I wasn't going to touch it." I glance back to the bedroom, wanting to get my cloak and run, even if it is in the dark. Although if we do… she may be waiting for us there. I don't know what's best. I don't know what to do.

"You don't have to do anything, Gretel. I'll take care of it," he says as if reading my mind.

"What do you mean? What are—"

Hansel's eyes harden. "I'm going to finish this place once and for all."

7

HANSEL

I'm done with this cottage and the fear it evokes. We burned the witch but this cottage... this cottage is cursed.

I take her face in both my hands and run my thumbs over her cheeks. Her lips. She stares up at me, her brow furrowed.

"Finish it?" she asks. "Hansel, what does that mean?"

"It means—this is over. This place won't exist. You can forget all about what happened. You can move on, and so can I, because this cottage won't be sitting here, haunting us."

"But—"

I cut her off with a kiss. Feeling a sense of purpose. This cottage will be nothing but ash.

The only thing I've ever been more sure of than my new quest is Gretel. Something changed in me when I laid eyes on her for the first time. Now I know what that was.

Gretel hesitates for a second, like she might argue with me about what I said, but then she melts into the kiss, parting her lips to let me in.

We fit together. That's the only way I can explain it. There's no awkwardness when I kiss her. There's no fumbling around, wondering what to do. I slide my hands down to her waist, holding the blanket close around her gorgeous body, and pull her close.

She's warm against me. The blanket brushes against my waist, and her breasts brush against my skin, and God—if I didn't have to *finish this*, I'd take her straight back to bed. If I didn't have family waiting for me in the village, I might never get out again.

Maybe someday, I'll have a bed of my own to give her. A house. A ring and life she deserves. Something other than all my bitterness and the old wounds from the witch.

Someday, when this cottage isn't here anymore. When it's scattered in the wind.

I break the kiss and pull her close, just holding her. I hate letting go so much I almost can't do it.

But then Gretel moves against me, taking a nervous little breath, and this can't wait. I should have done this the first time I came back here. I'd spent so many nights awake and sweating in my bed, wondering if the witch was really dead, and finally I came to find out.

Maybe she was waiting for the two of us. Maybe she really did lure Gretel here.

I press a kiss to Gretel's forehead, then let go. It's time to end this.

In here makes it feel like the chains might still be touching me. Those damned things are nowhere to be seen, so I can't drag them outside and melt them down.

But the rest?

The rest of this cottage is weak. It's just wood. It's made of things that can be destroyed if a man puts his mind to it, and I'm putting my mind to it.

I let myself loose.

I start by the sink in the kitchen, tearing dried herbs off the walls along with the boards the hooks were nailed into. I rip off a set of indoor shutters, then make a loop around the cottage, pulling off the rest. Shutters on the inside *and* the outside. The witch wanted to be able to hide. She never wanted anyone to find out what kind of things she did in here.

It's too bad for her that I found out. It's even worse that Gretel and I survived, because now I'm going to wipe this place out of existence.

Gretel watches me intently, staying close as I tip the wood into the fire. It leaps up around the boards like it's delighted to have something to blaze through.

I break down the chairs at the kitchen table. They go into the fire as well. The oven is roaring now, pouring heat into the house, but I don't want to feed that thing. The bedroom grate is better.

"*This* is what you should have burned," I say to the flames, though I know it wasn't *this fucking fire* that wiped out the crops and sent people to early graves from starvation. "This hellhole." She joins me in destruction, grabbing everything she can. The pillows and cushions. The drapes and the rugs.

Gretel comes with me when I head back for more pieces of the house. She grabs my arm as the fire catches and slips through the grate.

"Hansel," she says, her voice gentle. "Maybe we shouldn't—"

"We're going," I snap, then take a deep breath and look her in the eyes. "We're going, Gretel. I'm burning this place to the ground, and then we're leaving."

"That's not going to be enough."

I stop dead in the middle of the rug, my arms full of panels from the walls. The cottage is old enough, and it's been sitting here long enough, that pieces are coming away in my hands almost as easily as the shutters.

"What do you mean, it's not going to be enough? This place *won't exist*. We—we *replaced* her. We replaced what happened with what we did. There's nothing left but to get rid of it. The memories though... what she did to you... what she did to you was—"

"Me?" Gretel has tears in her eyes. Her chin, which she'd stuck out so bravely, wobbles. "I can't stand to see what she did to *you*."

"Gretel." I bend down and kiss her temple, then her cheek. "The worst part about that night was seeing you cry. I would have survived anything she threw at me to be able to take you home, and it was —God. You screaming for me like that—nothing could be worse. Do you understand? Nothing. I can't let her do that to you again."

"She *tortured* you," Gretel argues, her voice breathless. She clears her throat. The fire rages behind her in the bedroom. Our time is running out. "She tortured you, Hansel. Why do you think I'm willing to let her live? I'm not going to let her—let her *taunt* me. She can't spend the rest of her life trying to scare me into anything. We *have* to kill her. Or I have to kill her. She has to be dead. That witch can't exist in the same world as us anymore. I can't take it."

"I love you, Gret. I always have."

Shock shows in her widened eyes and for a moment it's like I cut her deep. Or like I kissed her for the first time. The sound is so packed with emotion that I can't decide what it means.

Gretel wouldn't have let me touch her if she didn't feel just as strongly. If she didn't trust me with every part of her.

She cares about me so much that she wants me out of here, just so being within these walls doesn't cause me any more pain. The fire cracks in the other room and it catches both of our attention.

"If we're going to leave, then we should leave now."

It's not enough though. Not enough to burn every last scrap in this nightmare. I stalk past Gretel and drop the next pile onto the flames.

There's still no sign of the witch and I'm

convinced as I toss the dishes in the flames that it is the house. This cottage is damned with baneful magic.

I wasn't strong enough when I was younger. I'm strong enough now. I've pushed all my anger deep down inside and saved it up so it could become strength.

"We can pretend," she insists. "We don't have to think about this place anymore, whether its here or not. When we go back home—"

"I'm not going back home while this cottage is still standing."

Gretel's huge eyes follow me as I go for another round. "Hansel, please. We can go right now. We can —we can talk. We can regroup. We need to make a plan to find her and kill her, and then—"

"This first."

"She could be coming for us right now."

"And?" Ripping the house apart feels like it's meant to be. Like I have to do it. It's a release I didn't know I needed until it was happening. "She could have come for us any time, if that's true."

"You really think she's dead?" she questions and I do. In the depths of my soul I know we banished her from existence. Whatever this is, this magic, it's something else.

"I know she's dead! I killed her. *We* killed her. We put her in the oven and burned the body. I know she's dead. I know she's gone. And now her house will be gone, too."

Gretel presses her lips together, silencing her protest and hurries for the table. She stacks the remaining plates and bowls into her arms and carries them into the bedroom, then dumps it all on the fire.

"Thought you said we had to leave," I say as she rushes back across the cottage.

"I'm not leaving without you. And if you really mean it—"

"I *do* really mean it. God, Gret, why else would I have come here? I want you to stop thinking about that night. It's never coming back."

"If you mean it," Gretel says, louder. "Then I'm helping you, because I don't think we have time."

"Nobody's coming. She's dead."

"We don't know that. And there's clearly magic here. The fires—"

"Can't be from her if she's dead."

"If she's alive, the magic might have called her here!"

I catch Gretel around the waist and pull her in

for a fierce kiss. When we break apart, she's gasping, a deep flush in her cheeks.

"If she comes here, she'll die," I tell her. "I'll kill her again with my own two hands. But dead people don't come back, Gretel. They just don't. There's no magic in the world that can bring an evil witch back from the grave."

"She didn't have a grave," says Gretel. "She went into the oven."

"Back from the oven, then."

"I really think we should go."

"And we will," I promise her. "Just as soon as this is done."

Gretel helps me as much as she can. The dishes take up a lot of space in the hearth, so after a few more trips, I have to wrench open the oven door.

It's much hotter than the bedroom fire and chews through wood in a few seconds.

I get one of the window frames out, and a gust of cold air whirls across my face. Somehow, I'll burn all my memories along with this cottage.

Gretel stops, bracing one hand against the wall and breathing deep.

"Let's just go," she pleads, one more time. "Let's just get the wagon ready and go. We can—"

She's interrupted by a loud crack of thunder.

Gretel jerks upright, staring at the ceiling. The next second, rain pours down on the roof. The wind *howls*. My pulse races and something has changed. I can feel it in my bones.

"Thunder," she shouts. Her eyes are wide with fear when they meet mine. Thunder isn't right. It's the middle of winter. It's not the right time of year for a thunderstorm, and no hot air came to mix with the cold, which has to mean—

"Gretel," I shout.

The door of the cottage opens wide. The firelight from the oven dims.

A figure at the door is illuminated in a flash of lightning. Cold scrapes down my spine. *Lightning* is just as wrong as thunder, but it's the figure at the door that stops my breath.

It's a witch.

It's *the* witch.

It's her. Fear used to paralyze me but in this moment every muscle in my body tightens. Every fiber of my being is prepared to fight. To defend Gretel.

I open my mouth to call out to her, to tell her to get behind me, but the witch waves a hand. When I shout Gretel's name, no sound comes out. Gretel's face is in shadow, but I can see her mouth moving.

She's trying to speak to me, but I can't hear a word she says.

Fear races through my veins as my body chills.

We've been silenced by magic. I can feel the spell in my throat, trapping my voice.

No. This isn't fucking happening. Not to us. Not again.

She's dead. She's supposed to be dead.

I run toward Gretel, but I've only gone two steps when the witch waves her hand again. Another spell. This one paralyzes me in place. I fight against it with all my strength, but I'm no match for the magic.

Gretel leaps toward me, light on her feet and her hands stretched out in front of her. If she can get to me, there's still hope. If the witch leaves her alone, then I'll survive somehow.

It's only a second or two, but it feels like forever until Gretel's fingertips touch me.

Her eyes come to mine, and then—

It's like she's gone.

Frozen. A statue. All of her, turned to stone.

8
GRETEL

*A*nother bolt of lightning comes down. It's so close to the cottage that it blinds me. All I can do is blink until the spots clear. My heart is a dull pounding, like everything has slowed. And yet it pains for Hansel.

Tears prick but don't fall. Fear exists but it's silenced.

I can't move. I can't move *at all*. This isn't like being frozen in place by fear, or trying to stay still during a game of hide-and-seek.

This is being frozen by *magic*.

I don't know how I'm still alive. I don't know how a body can *be* this still and keep living.

Am I going to die?

I try to curl my fingers, then my toes. I can't do either. I try to flex my hands. Not that, either. Time is slowed and yet I can do nothing.

Panic swells inside my chest, but it has nowhere to go. I can't run to let it out. I can't scream. I can't do anything but stand here, barely touching Hansel.

But I can blink, and if I try, I can move my gaze to look around the cottage.

As I focus, the vision on the door becomes clear.

She's a beautiful witch. Her gown is flowing and pale, and looks too light for the winter. At the same time, it looks sturdy and warm. I can't tell which is real, or if the dress is an illusion.

Is *she* an illusion?

If she is, she's a kind one. Her expression is kind, and her eyes are kind. There is no malice in her face at all. That might not mean anything. The witch had looked kind in the beginning as well. She had offered us sweets and shelter. She had seemed harmless until she shut the door and refused to let us leave.

But then her face had transformed, and all her hatred was there on the surface.

This witch though, her expression is calming. Even as I stand entranced, the fear dims.

I watch for signs of it on the beautiful witch's face, but there are none. She smiles gently at us, then glances around the cottage, seeming to see it for the first time.

This witch looks nothing like the witch who hurt Hansel, and who I thought was going to hurt me. She doesn't seem familiar with this place the way the evil witch had. This was her home, after all, so it would make sense that another witch wouldn't know it.

Unless she's pretending.

I can hear my pulse rushing in my ear. I need answers, and I need them badly, or else I might faint.

I'm not *completely* frozen, I realize. I'm still breathing. So is Hansel. We have our lungs, at least.

The beautiful witch doesn't seem to be in a hurry to speak to us. I don't know what that means. Is it because she has her prey where she wants us, or because we're not prey at all?

God, I want to know.

The witch waves her hand and the flames dim, what once was burned comes back whole and finds it's place around us. The damage we did is undone. In only a wave of her hand, the rage and harm against the cottage is reversed. In a blink of an eye, it's as if nothing happened. The flames in the fire crack and then subside to a warmed inferno. A nonthreatening and comforting heat. She waves her hand again, still silent and observing.

The light from the oven's open door brightens again. Whatever spell paralyzed me falls away, and I throw myself into Hansel's arms. He folds them around me and holds on tight.

"Gretel," he whispers, too quiet for the witch to hear and with no voice behind it. I don't think he can make a sound.

I clear my throat, but that doesn't make any sound, either. I cling hard to Hansel's shirt.

The witch waves her hand again, and the door closes behind her. The wall behind us rattles, and the spaces Hansel made around the window close up, stopping the frigid draft. She pats at her hair, shakes out her shoulders, and folds her hands in front of her, looking between us as if we're her guests. The light cloak around her seems to drift in a wind that doesn't exist as she moves towards us.

"Hansel and Gretel, I presume?"

I nod, although I do not want to. My body obeys the powerful being.

We'll get through this, I promise myself. *We'll both get through this.*

Hansel's hands spread out on my back as if he can hear my thoughts. We *will* get through this, but Hansel's heart is pounding in his chest. He's tense, and obviously doesn't trust her. I don't trust her, either.

She bows her head, accepting my answer, then looks at us once more, an apologetic slant to her mouth.

"I do apologize for the silencing, but I've found mortals don't respond well to unexpected visitors. You didn't care for the candlelight and the supper." The witch gives a shrug, looking slightly disappointed at how we treated the food. She adds, her brow perking, "I thought they were delicious, myself."

I don't know what to do. Tears well in my eyes. My heart races, all out of rhythm. The feeling I get from this woman is one of safety and peace, but how can I be sure of that?

I have Hansel's arms around me. For now, that has to be enough.

It's a small comfort. It lets my heart settle down a bit, beating softer. It's still going far too fast.

Moment by moment. Question by question.

The witch studies us, then lets out a quiet sigh. A flick of her hand, and the cottage is transformed. All the dark, dusty wood is replaced with whitewashed plaster walls. Fresh flowers spring into a vase near the sink.

Fresh flowers, in the middle of winter. If I cared to let go of Hansel, I would go over and touch them, because—

They're impossible.

The iron oven disappears. A cozy fireplace appears in the wall where the oven used to be.

This is *all* impossible. For a moment I question my sanity and if I've slipped into the depths of sleep again.

But it's all real. I know it in my heart. I don't know if I can stand another heartbreak. It would be one too many, and for Hansel...

I don't think Hansel could stand it, either. I think he might finish tearing the cottage to the ground no matter how many times this witch repairs it.

He might insist on trying for the rest of his life.

I wouldn't blame him for that, either.

The witch glances around and smiles at her work. "That's better. Perhaps I should have redecorated *before* you came. Though...I also know what you did before, and I couldn't risk that, could I?"

Neither of us can answer, and I don't move. I just want to stay close to Hansel and feel his heartbeat.

I've needed him so much since my father took me away, and now every second I have to touch him is worth—

It's worth more than anything to me. It's worth my life. I don't have an answer for the witch, anyway.

She glances between Hansel and I, her lips pursed, then seems to make a decision.

"You there." With a graceful hand, she points at me. "Gretel. Speak."

The magic she had used to silence me fades. I hadn't realized I could feel it in my throat and only notice it once it's gone.

"Please." I'll never say anything more important. I don't care about myself. I just need her to leave Hansel in peace. Although *Hansel* cares about me. I should beg for my life, but my throat is too tight. My voice is too raw. I love him too much. "Please don't hurt him."

The witch's face softens, and she lifts one hand as if she wants to touch us, to comfort us.

"Oh, sweet child, I don't intend to hurt either of you. This—" She gestures around at the now-gorgeous cottage, encompassing the door to the bedroom, too. "Does this look like pain to you?"

Tears of hope prick my eyes although I don't

trust the relief her words promise. I can't speak, though the spell no longer stops me. Of course it doesn't *look* like pain. It looks beautiful. But the cottage had not looked truly dangerous before. I don't know how to trust anything anymore. I don't know how to trust her.

The witch seems to sense that, because her gaze turns even kinder.

"It is not," she says reassuringly. "This is *healing*."

"Healing?" I choke out in blasphemy. I can't deny that some of the time we've spent here *has* been healing. It was at least a gift I'll be grateful for as long as I live. I didn't even *want* to live this much before Hansel opened the door and let me inside. I would have been so lonely without him. "You brought us here to heal?"

"You brought yourselves here," she answers gently. "But…I may have helped you along."

"Did you—you left those stones at my house, didn't you? You left them on the path, and you left them in my living room so I *had* to see them."

"I did," she confirms, looking only a little sheepish. "But I promise to you—I had no evil intent."

My throat closes, and I can't speak. *I thought she was coming back. I thought I had brought her back to the village, and I couldn't live with that. I'd already lost my father, and I'd lost Hansel, and I couldn't lose what was left of my life again.*

"I do have sorrow that I have caused you pain," the witch says. It sounds like a true, sincere apology, with real sorrow in her voice. "I did not wish to frighten you. I only desired to right the wrongs that had been done."

"You're not her, then?" Hansel says brusquely. He doesn't sound afraid although his voice is rough and low. He sounds as if he's still ready to defend me from *anything*—even magic. I'm more in love with him than ever, and I've loved Hansel for as long as I can remember.

"I am not the witch who dwelled here before," the beautiful witch answers. "She is dead, and will not return. But the damage she did to both of you has lingered, and deserves to be repaired. I felt that the two of you needed to return to this place to see that you had grown in spite of what happened here, and I feared that without a hand to guide you, you would never come to that conclusion on your own."

"Repair?" I echo, my mind working slowly after the rush of adrenaline and fear.

"You are meant to be together." Her bright blue eyes stare through me. "There is no one on earth who is better suited to either of you, and I cannot let that precious love die from the harms of that evil creature. It is my duty and honor to do what I can to offer true love a chance to survive, and to grow."

Tears slip down my cheeks. I watch through blurry vision as the witch takes something from around her neck.

It is an amulet with a dark red gem shining on the surface. I recognize it immediately and all hope is paused. My heart misses a beat at the sight of it. The beautiful witch holds it up in the light, and as we watch, it snaps in two in her hands.

She drops the pieces to the floor, but they disappear before they land.

"Was that keeping her away?" I ask, my voice shaking with emotion. "You don't mean for us to face her, do you?"

"She is gone," the witch promises. "I have not lied to you. The amulet represented the harm she did in her living years, and now I hope you will be able to let go of the pain she caused you here. There is still good in the world, after all—and the most powerful magic is love. You carry that between you wherever you go."

Hansel straightens, like he's just waking up. "You aren't here to punish us? There's no one to fight?"

The witch steps closer and puts her hand to his

cheek. She does the same to mine and looks into my eyes, then returns her gaze to Hansel. "You've been fighting all this time. The battle is over."

Hansel makes a rough sound. "So you'll let us go?" he questions.

She nods solemnly. "You were only children back then," the witch says. Her eyes are so kind. There is nothing in her touch that speaks of the evil witch. "You can let it go now. You can have your happily ever after."

"Thank you," I whisper, and close my eyes, unshed tears spilling. Relief spreads through me although a part of me will not trust her until we are gone.

Hansel holds me tighter. I inhale, trying not to cry, and when I exhale, the heat of the witch's hand is gone.

I open my eyes.

The witch is gone, too. The cottage is quiet around us apart from the cracking of the fire, and remains transformed. It's bright and clean with a basket of apples on the table and a pastry cooling in a dish near the sink.

But it's the glass jar on the windowsill that catches my eye. The firelight reflects off of it, and inside—

"Hansel," I manage to say. "Look."

"What is it?" he says into my hair.

I turn both of us so he can look without letting go of me. Hansel's eyes move over the room and all the transformations the witch made in the blink of an eye.

He takes a quick breath when he sees the jar and guides me closer, one hand steady on my waist, the other reaching out for the jar. His hand trembles as he lifts the lid and sets it carefully aside, then reaches in.

He plucks one of the pieces from the jar, folds it in his fingers, and smiles down at it.

Then he holds it in front of me and opens his hand.

There, in his palm, is a perfect twist of pure white wax paper, wrapped lovingly around a piece of orange-and-yellow taffy.

It's the color of the sunrise. It's the color of a brand-new day.

"I need you Gretel," Hansel whispers. "Please stay with me forever."

Lifting my chin I look deep into his eyes, "I'll never leave you ever again. I love you."

As he kisses me, I hold him like he's mine forevermore. Because he is.

He was always the love of my life.

He breaks the kiss and breathes deeply, repeating over and over, "I love you."

If you're a fan of fantasy, retellings and Greek Mythology my Hades and Persephone retelling, His in The Dark is available now!

ABOUT WILLOW WINTERS

Thank you so much for reading my romances. I'm just a stay at home mom and avid reader turned author and I couldn't be happier.

I hope you love my books as much as I do!

To browse more of my books, visit https://willowwinterswrites.com/pages/reading-order

THE DISCREET SERIES

This is the Discreet Edition so no-one knows what you are reading.

You can find more here
https://willowwinterswrites.com/collections/
discreet-series